MW01042284

Aa Bb Cc
Dd Ee Ff
Gg Hh Ii Jj
Kk Ll Mm

It was the first day of school, and Sam felt some jitters.
He'd be meeting new people and all sorts of critters!
His mom said, "Don't worry! You'll discover new friends.
You'll share stories and laughter, and time you will spend."

Sam snatched up his backpack and SLAMMED the front door.
"I'm leaving to go meet new friends and explore!"
But to Sam's shock while walking to class,
he spied a **congregation of alligators**, praying at mass!

Bb

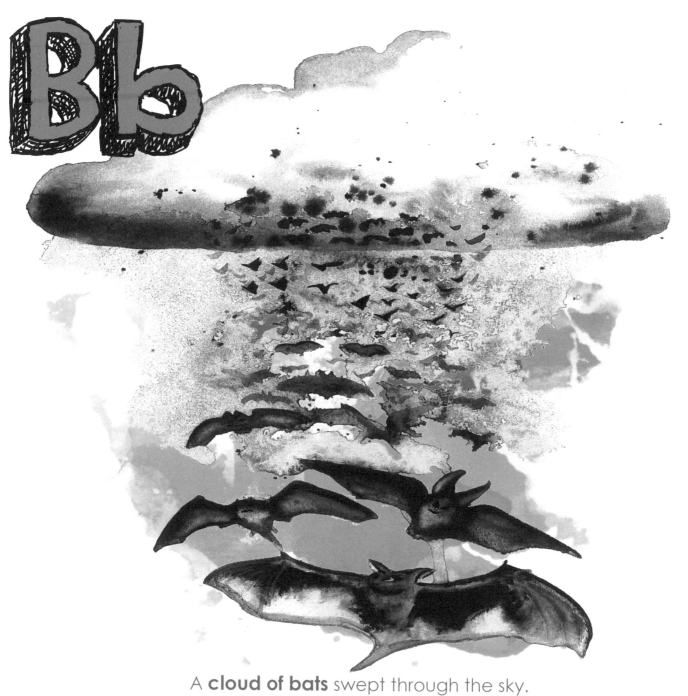

A **cloud of bats** swept through the sky.
Sam could see them swoop and fly.
Bats are nocturnal, hunting at night,
the only mammals capable of continuous flight.

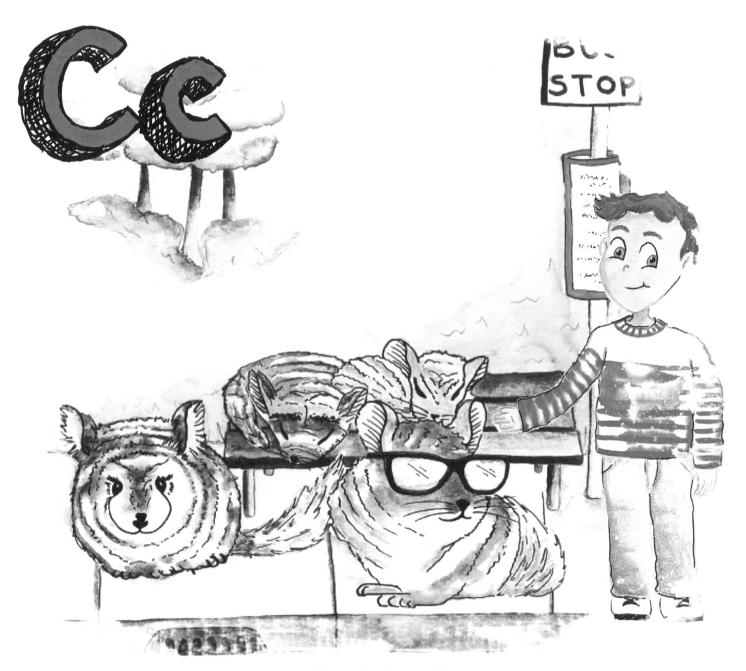

Sam continued along his route.
"My, this has been a strange commute."
At the bus stop, he heard something screech:
a **colony of chinchillas** chin-chillin' on the street!

Sam wondered if he would find his crew.
"This is more of a walk in the zoo!"
He heard some beats that were strange to his ear:
it was a full on rap battle by a **gang of deer**!

5

Ee

Sam didn't think deer was where he belonged,
so he continued his journey along to the pond.
There was a splash of water, which beyond any doubt,
was a **memory of elephants** dancing about!

Now that Sam's T-shirt had got a bit wet
he was happy he wasn't at school just quite yet!
Stopping for lollypops might have its merits,
but Sam had been beat by a **business of ferrets**!

Gg

Sam returned to the city street
wondering what other species he'd meet.
A **tower of giraffes** stood proud and tall,
making Sam feel rather small.

8

Hh

Sam continued past city towers,
and came to a garden with beautiful flowers.
Twinkles of color began to zig and to zag.
It was a **charm of hummingbirds** playing tag!

Sam was wondering if it was his fate
to roll in to the first day of school very late.
But up came a roadblock Sam didn't expect,
a swarming, buzzing **plague of insects**!

10

Sam passed the aquarium, the best place to be!
Home of the creatures that live in the sea.
Like upside down umbrellas, almost identical,
swam a **smack of jellyfish** waving their tentacles.

Kk

"The critters show no signs of stopping!"
Here they come in a hip and a hopping!
A baby in a pouch shouted "YAHOO!"
Cuddled amongst a **mob of kangaroos**.

Sam could see cacti and the air become hot,
"I think I'm in the desert!" Sam thought.
Peering over sand dunes, Sam took a look.
It was a **lounge of lizards** reading some books!

13

Mm

Sam continued to the forested path,
he could hear squeaking and devilish laughs.
There were piles of paper, leaves and debris.
It was a **mischief of mice** toilet papering a tree!

Nn

Peering deep down the blue ocean wall,
Sam spied a **blessing of purple narwhals**.
He heard the clicking of underwater predation.
Toothed whales hunt by echolocation.

15

The next group of animals that Sam could spy
were staring at him with sharp yellow eyes!
With plumage and feathers and talons and claws,
a **parliament of owls** were discussing the law!

16

A bicyclist had taken a spill
after riding upon a tail of quills!
This unfortunate trick had been conspired
by a **prickle of porcupines** who popped his bike tire.

Qq

Sam continued along the trail,
and came across a **covey of quail**.
Rustling their feathers and shifting their legs
to warm and protect their family of eggs.

A **crash of rhinos** were racing to town,
swerving and veering in a car that they found.
The car hit a tree with a bang and some screeches!
Down came tumbling a group of peaches.

Ss

Sam could hear a tumultuous fuss,
and wondered what was kicking up piles of dust.
There were beats and songs, someone was jammin'.
Crossing the finish line — a **run of salmon**!

Tt

Stalking their prey, came an **ambush of tigers**.
a fresh piece of meat, one of their desires.
Although, thought Sam, candy is sweeter,
ligers and tigers are strictly meat eaters.

21

Uu

Sam walked up to the school gym
where teams paused at halftime, discussing their win.
With rainbow flow hair and pointed sharp horns,
dribbled a **team of unicorns**.

Vv

The walk to school had not gone as planned.
Sam came upon a castle of sand,
where, with tails that moved like windshield wipers,
slithered an entire **generation of vipers**!

The day was slipping away, and Sam had yet to learn,
so he stopped by a **bed of sleeping roundworms**.
He listened to books and nursery rhymes,
as these slumbering worms liked to share story time.

24

Sam wasn't the only creature ready for school,
he passed by a glittering mass in the pool.
X-ray tetra fish schools live in the Amazon,
insects are what they typically feed on.

Sam's excitement he could hardly contain
as he gazed upon the mountain plain.
Picking through rocks was a **herd of yaks**,
grazing on grass and berries as snacks!

Sam couldn't believe it — he'd made it to school!
A **crossing of zebras** were following the rules
by stopping at the crosswalk, and looking both ways,
ensuring their safety and ongoing play!

The teacher cried, "Sam! Where have you been?"
Sam replied, "Meeting all kinds of marvelous friends!
My kind includes all beasts — scaled, feathered or furry!
Creatures that slither, swim, trot, fly or scurry!"

"These groupings of animals, I've come to see,
have to be protected by you and me!
For this big tribe of earthlings, we have to show care.
For the animal families, and the planet we share."

29

Author:
Shayna Campbell

Artist:
Jana Champagne

Shayna Campbell is a pharmacist from St. Albert, Alberta, Canada who has been rhyming poems from an early age. She loves exploring the natural world around her in the Rocky Mountains and beyond. Shayna wanted to share her love of animals with her niece and nephews and hopes they too will develop a curiosity and respect for our shared earthling creatures. Shayna's favourite animal group is a pod of orca whales.

Jana Champagne is a product developer and graphic designer from St. Paul, Alberta, Canada. Her artistic eye and love of beautifying the world around her impacts all of her projects from children's outerwear pieces ukulele musical numbers to ski and snowboard lines. Jana was inspired to create these paintings for her nieces and nephews as she was curious what her overall painting style would be. Jana's favourite animal group is a clowder of cats.

Thank You!

Nn Oo Pp
Qq Rr Ss Tt
Uu Vv Ww
Xx Yy Zz

CPSIA information can be obtained
at www.ICGtesting.com
Printed in the USA
LVHW072037241120
672394LV00002B/17